IN THE ATTIC

Text copyright © 1984 by Hiawyn Oram. Illustration copyright © 1984 by Satoshi Kitamura
This paperback edition first published in 2004 by Andersen Press Ltd. The rights of Hiawyn Oram and Satoshi Kitamura
to be identified as the author and illustrator of this work have been asserted by them in accordance with the Copyright,
Designs and Patents Act, 1988. First published in Great Britain in 1984 by Andersen Press Ltd., 20 Vauxhall Bridge Road,
London SW1V 2SA. Published in Australia by Random House Australia Pty., 20 Alfred Street, Milsons Point,
Sydney, NSW 2061. Printed and bound in Italy by Grafiche AZ, Verona. All rights reserved.

10 9 8 7 6 5 4 3 2 1

British Library Cataloguing in Publication Data available.

ISBN 1 84270 358 7

This book has been printed on acid-free paper

IN THE ATTIC

TEXT BY
HIAWYN ORAM
PICTURES BY
SATOSHI KITAMURA

AN E_SEN PRESS LON ON

I had a million toys and I was bored.

I climbed into the attic.

I was there now.

The attic was empty. Or was it?

I found a family of mice.

and a colony of beetles and a cool,

quiet place to rest and think.

I met a spider and we made a web.

I opened a window that opened other windows.

I found an old engine and I made it work.

I went out to look for someone to share

what I had found

and found a friend.

My friend and I found a game that could

go on forever because it kept changing.

I climbed out of the attic and told my mother
where I'd been all day.
"But we don't have an attic," she said.

Well, she wouldn't know, would she?

She hasn't found the ladder.

Another exhilarating read
from Hiawyn Oram and Satoshi Kitamura

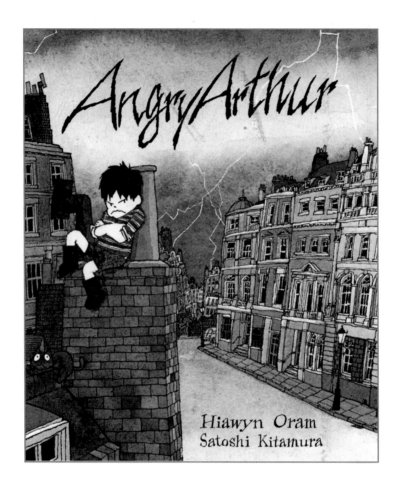

Winner of the Mother Goose Award

'An important book, a brilliant one even, on something known to
every child but not much spoken about - deep frustrated rage.'
Times Educational Supplement

'Satoshi Kitamura sweeps all before him.' *Bookseller*

'Children will love it.' *Guardian*

'A brilliant book.' *Observer*'

ISBN 0 86264 017 2   £ 9.99

A highly original alphabet book from Satoshi Kitamura

'There could be no better way to start than with Kitamura's wonderful illustrations.'
Observer

'The bold, bright, beautiful style of Satoshi Kitamura stands out like a beacon.'
Times Educational Supplement

'Highly recommended as a creative way to explore the alphabet.'
Early Years Educator

ISBN 1 84270 756 8   £ 4.99

More Andersen Press paperback picture books!

What Kind of Monster?
by Mark Birchall

Our Cat Flossie
by Ruth Brown

Charlotte's Piggy Bank
by David McKee

King Smelly Feet
by Hiawyn Oram and John Shelley

Millie's Big Surprise
by Gerald Rose

Mrs Goat and Her Seven Little Kids
by Tony Ross

Frog Finds a Friend
by Max Velthuijs

New Shoes
by Jeanne Willis and Margaret Chamberlain